The Bad-Tempered Ladybird

Eric Carle

PUFFIN

It was night, and some fireflies danced around the moon.

At five o'clock in the morning the sun came up.
A friendly ladybird flew in from the left. It saw a leaf with many aphids on it,
and decided to have them for breakfast.
But just then a bad-tempered ladybird flew in from the right.
It too saw the aphids and wanted them for breakfast.

"Good morning," said the friendly ladybird.
"Go away!" shouted the bad-tempered ladybird. "I want those aphids."
"We can share them," suggested the friendly ladybird.
"No. They're mine, all mine," screamed the bad-tempered ladybird.
"Or do you want to fight me for them?"

"If you insist," answered the friendly ladybird sweetly.
It looked the other ladybird straight in the eye.
The bad-tempered ladybird stepped back.
It looked less sure of itself.
"Oh, you're not big enough for me to fight," it said.
"Then why don't you pick on somebody bigger?"
"I'll do that!" screeched the bad-tempered ladybird.
"I'll show you!" It puffed itself up and flew off.

At six o'clock
it met a wasp.
"Hey you," said
the bad-tempered
ladybird.
"Want to fight?"
"If you insist," said
the wasp,
showing its stinger.
"Oh, you're not
big enough," said
the bad-tempered
ladybird
and flew off.

At five o'clock
it met a whale.
"Hey you," said
the bad-tempered
ladybird.
"Want to fight?"
But the whale
didn't answer at all.
"You're not
big enough anyway," said
the bad-tempered ladybird
and flew off.

At four o'clock
it encountered
an elephant.
"Hey you," said
the bad-tempered ladybird.
"Want to fight?"
"If you insist," said the elephant,
raising its trunk and
showing its big tusks.
"Oh, you're not big enough,"
said the bad-tempered ladybird
and flew off.

At three o'clock
it ran into
a rhinoceros.
"Hey you," said
the bad-tempered
ladybird.
"Want to fight?"
"If you insist," said
the rhinoceros,
lowering its horn.
"Oh, you're not big enough,"
said the bad-tempered
ladybird
and flew off.

At two o'clock
it met a gorilla.
"Hey you," said
the bad-tempered ladybird.
"Want to fight?"
"If you insist," said the gorilla,
beating its chest.
"Oh, you're not big enough,"
said the bad-tempered ladybird
and flew off.

At one o'clock
it happened upon
a hyena.
"Hey you," said
the bad-tempered ladybird.
"Want to fight?"
"If you insist," said the hyena,
laughing eerily and
showing its teeth.
"Oh, you're not big enough,"
said the bad-tempered ladybird
and flew off.

At five fifteen the bad-tempered ladybird said to one of the whale's flippers, "Hey you, want to fight?"

But it got no answer. So it flew on.

At five thirty the bad-tempered ladybird said to the whale's fin, "Hey you, want to fight?"

But it got no answer. So it flew on.

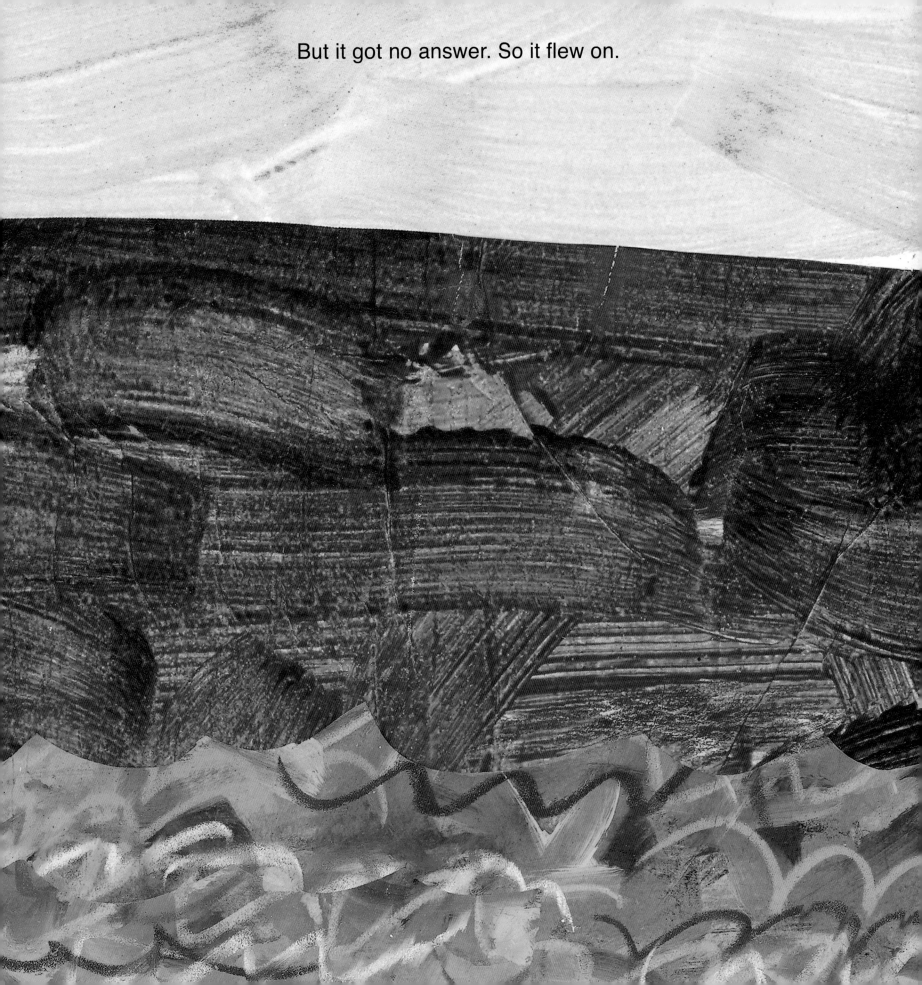

At a quarter to six the bad-tempered ladybird said to the whale's tail, "Hey you, want to fight?"

. . . that it flew across the sea and across the land.

At six o'clock the bad-tempered ladybird arrived right back where it had started from.

"Ah, here you are again," said the friendly ladybird. "You must be hungry. There are still some aphids left. You can have them for dinner."
"Oh, thank you," said the wet, tired and hungry ladybird.

Soon all the aphids were gone.
"Thank you," said the leaf.
"You are welcome," answered both the ladybirds, and they went to sleep.
The fireflies, who had been sleeping all day, came out to dance around the moon.